The Great McGoniggle's Gray Ghost

The Great McGoniggle's Gray Ghost

by
SCOTT CORBETT

Illustrated by *Bill Ogden*

An Atlantic Monthly Press Book

Little, Brown and Company
BOSTON   TORONTO

FIRST EDITION

T 10/75

Library of Congress Cataloging in Publication Data

Corbett, Scott.
  The Great McGoniggle's gray ghost.

  "An Atlantic Monthly Press book."
  SUMMARY: Two boys attempt to recover a balloon bearing
a valuable prize certificate which has become attached to
the eaves of a mansion inhabited by a disagreeable couple
and a ferocious dog.
  I. Ogden, William. II. Title.
PZ7.C79938Gt   [Fic]   75-17722
ISBN 0-316-15725-2

ATLANTIC-LITTLE, BROWN BOOKS
ARE PUBLISHED BY
LITTLE, BROWN AND COMPANY
IN ASSOCIATION WITH
THE ATLANTIC MONTHLY PRESS

Published simultaneously in Canada
by Little, Brown & Company (Canada) Limited

PRINTED IN THE UNITED STATES OF AMERICA

To Bert, Rolly, and the Boys

1.

Mac McGoniggle was looking through the field glasses when Eddie Becker came along. Mac and Ken were standing on a hillside in the park.

"Hi, Eddie," said Ken.

"Hi," said Eddie. "What are you guys doing? Bird watching?"

"No," said Mac. "Balloon watching."

Ken felt foolish, but nothing ever seemed to make Mac feel that way. It did not bother him one bit to have a wise guy like Eddie Becker catch them doing something that looked silly.

"Balloon watching?" Eddie snorted. "What are you talking about?"

Mac lowered the glasses and gave Eddie a patient look, as though he were about to explain something serious and sensible to someone who was not too bright.

"You heard about all those balloons they turned loose yesterday?"

"Sure, who didn't?"

"Well, the prevailing wind is southwesterly, so I figure a lot of them must have blown this way."

Eddie's reaction to that was predictable. Another snort.

"Fat chance. Even if they did they've probably all come down somewhere by now."

"Maybe. But it doesn't cost anything to look."

The new Belmont Shoppers Mall on the other side of town had opened the day before with great fanfare. As a publicity gimmick a hundred balloons had been released, each with a waterproof plastic envelope hooked onto the end of its string. The envelopes contained gift certificates.

All at once Eddie changed his tune. He

pointed excitedly and his voice sharpened with instant greed.

"Hey! There's a balloon now! I saw it first!"

"Gee, you're right! We'll go halvers!" Mac shouted after Eddie, who was already racing down the slope of the hill, determined to be first on the scene when the balloon finally came down.

"Nothing doing!" yelled Eddie over his shoulder. "I saw it first!"

Mac watched him go and chuckled wickedly.

Back in the days before he had fallen in with the Great McGoniggle, Ken Wetzel would probably have spoiled everything by saying something like, "Aw, we already spotted that one, Eddie, and when you look at it through the glasses you can see it hasn't got anything on the end of its string. It's the kind they sell over by the refreshment stand. Probably got away from some little kid. We've seen four of them already."

But now all Ken did was grin and say, "McGoniggle, you're a rat. That will probably come down miles from here."

"Well, the exercise will do him good, the greedy jerk," said Mac. "I just wish it looked more like a Gray Ghost, so he'd really get excited."

Gray Ghosts, according to the Mall's publicity, were the balloons that carried the most valuable certificates. Red ones carried $5 certificates, blue $10, green $25, and gray, the hardest to spot, carried $50 certificates.

In spite of the satisfactory way they had disposed of Eddie Becker, Ken was still feeling foolish. Balloon watching in the park!

"Of all the crazy ways to spend Sunday afternoon," he grumbled, thinking that a lot of the time he passed in Mac's company was spent in crazy ways — crazy maybe, but never boring. "Even if we spot one we'll never track it to where it comes down. And Eddie's probably right. They're all down by now."

"He forgot *that* idea in a hurry when he spotted something," Mac pointed out. "Okay, let's go home. I'm getting a stiff neck anyhow. Here, put 'em away."

Ken slipped the field glasses into the case slung across his chest and under his arm. The glasses belonged to his father. Whenever they needed special equipment it was usually Ken who provided it. Mac did not have much at home other than a father who was always changing to a more interesting job, a mother who worked part-time — a large part of her time — to help make ends meet, and two older sisters and a kid brother. His sisters had impressive names, Cordelia and Rosamund, and his kid brother was named Hubert.

In spite of not having much else they seemed to have a lot of fun in their small, shabby house. One time Ken had found the whole family dressed up in silly clothes, acting a wild melodrama they made up on the spot. Nothing like that ever went on in his house.

He was both glad and sorry his own parents were so sensible.

"Balloon watching! What'll you think of next?" Ken said aloud, and he knew that this question was one reason he hung around with McGoniggle so much.

2.

Ken Wetzel was of medium height and weight, average in his class at Chester P. Kilroy Junior High School, an ordinary, everyday boy.

Then he met the Great McGoniggle.

Since Mac had chosen him as his best friend Ken had found himself constantly involved in situations not average or everyday in any way. Life with McGoniggle was an education in the possibilities of surprise. And even though Mac sometimes made him nervous, Ken was becoming more and more willing to be surprised.

As for Mac, he was tall, thin, and wiry with a face that made people grin. He had a thin nose that turned up at the tip and the wide mouth of a clown, but there was an owlish look to his eyes, as though they were almost crossed from getting in each other's way. Mac did not miss anything. If there was a Gray Ghost to be found, he would find it. He would keep looking.

They had left the park and were walking along Grafton Street past a high stone wall. A tall, ornate Victorian mansion loomed behind the wall. A man stood facing a break in the wall, a stubby little old man with a bouquet of flowers clutched in one hand. He seemed to be arguing with someone on the other side of a pair of iron gates.

"But this is a public right-of-way!" he cried. "I've been using it to go to the cemetery for fifteen years!"

"Well, you're not going to use it any longer, so walk around to the main entrance," said an angry male voice from the other side of the gates.

"That's right," said a shrill voice with a

nasty edge to it. A woman's voice, it was a good match for the man's. "We're tired of having a lot of ragtag and bobtail tramping past our house every day, right through our grounds, and we're not going to put up with it any longer."

"You've got no right to shut the gates on Sunday!" insisted the old man. "The city won't let you get away with it!"

"That's what you think. It's only a few blocks around to the main entrance and the walk will do you good. For that matter, we're doing you a kindness by keeping these gates closed — because I'm warning you, if you ever try to sneak in this way from now on, Rufus here will tear you to bits!"

By now the boys could see the couple on the other side of the gates. They were gray-haired with thin, hard faces. The big dog sitting beside them was enough to give anybody the shudders. He made the Hound of the Baskervilles look like a lap dog and appeared quite capable of taking the seat out of anyone's pants, and maybe an extra dividend as well.

The couple turned on their heels and walked back toward the house, leaving the old man with the flowers muttering to himself. The big dog sat where he was, keeping an evil eye on him.

The old man needed an audience. When the

boys were passing the gates he swept an arm toward the house and burst into a tirade.

"Them two think they own the town! For fifteen years I been going through there, minding my own business, walking to the cemetery to put flowers on my wife's grave, and now they say I can't! They got no right!"

Mac cast an interested glance through the gates.

"Who are they?" he asked.

"Cyrus and Etta Simmons, curse 'em! Rich as Croesus, and twice as mean! They got no right — but they got money and lawyers, and they'll get away with it. You'll see, they'll get away with it!"

The old man shied away as the big dog suddenly snarled and rushed forward to jump against the gates, barking furiously and making the iron bars clang with his weight.

"Nice doggie!" said Mac, and grabbed Ken by the arm. "Here, I'll throw you a few bones. Not much meat on them, but —"

"He'd eat him, too! He's a mortal terror!"
said the old man, glaring at the animal. "He'd
tear you limb from limb, that one, if he got
the chance. Well, I guess there's nothing to do
but walk around the other way — and me

with a gimpy leg. My wife's grave is close to this side, so I'll have to walk all the way back across the cemetery as well. And all because of them two!"

Then he noticed the case slung under Ken's arm. He glanced at the big house and back at the boys.

"Say, sonny, is that a pair of spyglasses you've got there?"

"Yes, sir."

He glowered at the Simmons house again and then asked, "Mind if I have a look through them?"

"Why, no."

The old man jerked his head toward the other side of the street.

"Step across the way with me to my house, will you, boys?"

3.

The houses on the other side of Grafton Street made quite a contrast with the Simmons mansion. They were small and plain, very plain, with little space between them. They stood on a steep terrace that was four or five steps high, with two more steps leading up onto front porches.

Narrow flowerbeds filled the cramped level strip between the top of the terrace and the front of the house to which the old man led them. It was obvious to Ken that the flowers were tended with loving care. Ken noticed they were the same kind the old man was carrying. They followed him as he limped painfully up the chipped concrete steps. Under the doorbell was a hand-lettered card that read G. SWANSON, and over it were the numerals 17.

"Are you Mr. Swanson?" asked Mac.

"That's right. Gustav Swanson, and I've lived in this house for forty years, but *them* two don't even act like they ever saw me before," he said, shooting another resentful glance across the street. "Now, if you'll let me have them glasses . . ."

He squinted through them in the direction of the Simmons mansion.

"Yes, sir! Just as I thought. Clear as day. Them that has, gits!" he declared bitterly.

"Gets what?"

"Here, take a look. Look at the gutter near the corner of the house there, just above the third-story windows."

Mac took a look. His lips twitched, and he spoke in a triumphant tone of voice, pleased to have his theory about the prevailing south-westerly winds verified.

"Well, look who's here!" he said, and handed the field glasses to Ken.

Ken could understand now why Mr. Swanson had brought them over to his front porch. Down at street level the trees around the Simmons mansion would have concealed what they could now see.

Caught in the gutter was a grayish lump, wrinkled and lopsided, the size of a softball.

Dangling from it on a short string was a small, square plastic envelope.

"Hey!" said Ken. "It's a Gray Ghost!"

22

"You're darn tooting it is!" agreed Mr. Swanson. "I read all about it in the papers — seen it on TV, for that matter. It's one of them fifty-dollar ones — and *them* two git it!"

The old man's face worked. He looked ready to weep.

"When I think what I could do with that . . . I've got a daughter with three kids. Her husband's gone and she's having a real struggle. They live here with me and I help all I can, but . . . When I think what an extra fifty dollars would mean to her . . ."

But then he shook his head and pulled himself together, and patted Ken's shoulder absently.

"Well, thanks anyway, sonny. I was wondering if I was seeing things — it's been bothering me ever since I noticed it this morning."

"I'll bet it came down during the night," said Mac.

"Shouldn't be surprised, lad."

23

Mac was staring across the street at the Simmons mansion with a glint in his off-center eyes that Ken had learned to recognize.

"Do they leave Rufus outside at night?" he asked in an offhand way.

"The dog? No, they keep him inside most of the time. Of course, they let him out when he has to go, but — why?"

"I was just wondering," said Mac.

Mr. Swanson grunted unhappily.

"Well, sooner or later one of them two will happen to notice that thing — all they have to do is look out that upstairs window right beside it — and then they'll haul it in. Yes, sir, them that has, gits! Thanks for the use of the spyglasses, boys. I'd better start moving — it takes me a while."

Mr. Swanson limped down the steps, suddenly in a hurry, and started up the street, turning once to wave to them with the hand that wasn't holding the flowers.

Mac sat down on the top step, still concentrating his owlish stare on the Gray Ghost across the street. He reminded Ken of a general planning an attack.

"Hmm . . ." Mac murmured. It was exactly the sort of challenge that brought out the best — or the worst, depending on how you looked at it — in the Great McGoniggle.

"Now, wait a minute!" cried Ken. "What do you think you're going to do?"

Mac replied with his most evil giggle.

"Well, poor old Mr. Swanson can't get at it, so I guess we'll just have to fetch it down for him."

"What? Are you crazy? How can we do that?"

"I don't know, but there's no time to lose. Any minute now one of those old buzzards may notice it hanging there."

"So what are you going to do? March over there with a thirty-foot ladder —"

"Well, no. And not now. We'll just have to gamble on their not spotting it before evening. This is a job that had best be done under cover of darkness," declared Mac with another evil, laughing giggle.

"You *are* crazy!" said Ken, and was proud of his own powers of observation as he went on to say, "In case you haven't noticed, there's a streetlight right in front of those gates. If you tried to climb over, anybody inside or out could see you!"

Mac answered him with a calculating chuckle that brought Ken no comfort.

"Ain't it the truth?" he agreed. "But if that's a right-of-way to the cemetery, there are two ends to it. What say we go have a look at the other end?"

4.

"We're wasting our time," said Ken on their way to the main entrance to the cemetery. "If they've blocked off one end, I'll bet they've blocked off the other end, too."

"It won't hurt to have a look," said Mac, and his eyes had a stubborn expression now. "That's a public right-of-way through there, and the corner of the house practically hangs over it. There's no trespassing involved — or not much, anyway. In fact, we'd be doing a good deed. We'd be helping the Simmonses."

"What are you talking about?"

"Well, we'd be cleaning out their gutters for them."

Mac snickered gleefully and added, "Listen,

I like to see justice done. Mr. Swanson says them that has, gits, but I like to think that once in a while them that has gits taken."

Ken struggled with his conscience. He was beginning to be tempted. On the other hand . . .

"But even if we sneaked in there, Mac, we're not human flies or a couple of second-story men — third-story, I mean! We can't climb up to where that balloon is. So how —"

"Where there's a will, there's a way. Hey, write that down, that's pretty good!" cried Mac, pretending he had just made it up.

Ken glared at him.

"I suppose you've got some harebrained scheme . . ."

The Great McGoniggle shook his head.

"No," he admitted, "not yet. But I'm working on it!"

When they reached the main entrance to the cemetery Mac became wary.

"Mr. Swanson said his wife's grave was over near the other end of that right-of-way," he reminded Ken, "so we've got to be careful. No sense in letting him see us. He'd only wonder what we're up to."

"He wouldn't be the only one," snapped Ken, but all he got for his pains was a grin.

After several minutes' walk they spotted their man. He was a small gray figure in the distance, on his knees beside a grave. Mac stopped and pointed to one side. "Let's cut over that way."

They made a wide sweep around Mr. Swanson and sat down to wait on the cover of an imposing marble mausoleum. Mac stretched out on his back with his fingers laced under his head and squinted up at the blue sky. Ken sat and watched Mr. Swanson, feeling uncomfortable.

"Reminds me of my granddad," said Mac, "only it was the other way around — Grandpa keeled over one day on the loading platform at the plant where he worked, right in the middle of cracking a joke. Grandma's never missed a Sunday at the cemetery since. She really thought a lot of that old man." Mac sat up and added, almost to himself, it seemed, "And so did I. Well, let's see . . . Hey, he's leaving."

Mr. Swanson had gotten to his feet and was limping away, looking very weary.

"Now," said Mac. "Let's find this end of the right-of-way."

It was not hard to locate because the wall that bounded the back end of the cemetery matched the one that ran along Grafton Street. Obviously it marked the boundary of the Simmons property.

The gates that closed off the right-of-way at that end had a chain and padlock holding them together, but were not as tall as the ones on Grafton Street.

"A cinch," said Mac confidently. "So now we know we can get in. Now all we have to do is —"

"Sure! Figure out a way to float up the side of the house!"

"What? How's that again?"

The Great McGoniggle had whirled around to face Ken, and an idea was sparkling in his owlish eyes.

"Never mind!" he said. "I heard you the first time!"

He smacked his hands together.

"Set a thief to catch a thief!" he cried, and looked at his wristwatch. "Come on, we've got to get back to the park!"

5.

They made it in time. The man who sold pinwheels and kites and balloons was still there doing business from his two-wheeled portable stand. A tank of hydrogen was strapped to the side of it.

"We want one with plenty of gas in it," Mac told him.

Some people thought Mac had the look of a troublemaker and wanted no part of him. Others seemed to like him on sight. Fortunately, the balloon man belonged to the second group. He reached for the cluster of balloons that were floating above his stand, tugging at their strings, and selected a particularly plump specimen.

"I slipped on this one and put in some extra gas," he explained. "Okay?"

"Great. Thanks." Mac handed him a quarter, which probably represented most of the money he had in the world at that moment.

Once more they left the park, this time with Mac carrying a large red balloon that would have made any other boy his age self-conscious. Balloons were for little kids. But Mac was too intent on the caper he had in mind to let a little thing like that bother him.

"Your folks home, Ken?"

"No. Dad's playing golf with a client and Mom's playing tennis."

"Good. Then we'd better take this to your place. If Hubert got one look at our balloon, that would be the last of it."

"Okay," said Ken, "but . . . do you think it will really work?"

Mac snorted grandly.

"Of course it will work! The envelope is hooked onto a piece of wire, and the wire is folded over but not closed tight. I could see it as plain as day through the glasses. We can't miss!"

"But how are we going to *get* there? I can

35

just see us walking down the street and sneak-
ing through a cemetery at night carrying a big
red balloon!"

Mac pulled the balloon down to eye level
and considered it with a measuring glance.

"It isn't much bigger than a twenty-pound
turkey," he declared, "and a twenty-pound
turkey goes into a supermarket shopping bag
easily. All we have to do is carry it in a bag
and nobody will think a thing about it. They'll
think we're taking home some groceries."

"On Sunday night?"

"Don't let it worry you!"

Once Ken had located a ball of stout cord, a
piece of wire, and some supermarket shopping
bags, they spent a few busy moments in his
room.

First Mac bent the wire into a loop about
four inches in diameter. He tied the balloon's
string to one side of the loop and the cord to
the other. Then, holding the cord, he let the
balloon go up to the ceiling.

For a moment they admired the arrangement.

"Set a thief to catch a thief," said Mac, "and set a balloon to catch a balloon."

He stuck out one thumb to represent the wire hook the packet was attached to. With his other thumb and middle finger he made a loop. He slipped the looped fingers over his thumb, and pulled down.

"Like that," he said.

"That ought to do it," admitted Ken.

"Okay, now pick out the biggest shopping bag you can find and let's put it in."

The balloon went in all right, but it did not want to stay in. Every time they pushed it down it popped up again before they could close the bag. The trouble was, there was not enough bag left to fold over at the top.

"All right, there's more than one way to skin a cat or sack a balloon," said Mac. "We'll turn this bag upside down and put it inside another bag."

But none of the bags were large enough to go over the first one when it had the balloon in it.

Then Ken thought of a possibility.

"I know! Mom's got a string bag she uses sometimes, and it'll hold *any* grocery bag."

The string bag worked fine. And by now the balloon was weighted down with enough paper and string and cord and wire so that it didn't float around, at least not too much.

"The next problem is, where am I going to hide it till tonight?" said Ken.

"Under the bed."

"No good. I don't want to have to sneak it out of the house after my folks come home."

Mac glanced out the window, down at the backyard.

"Poor old Prince," he said, referring to the Wetzels' long departed dog. "I'm sorry he had to go, but you've still got his doghouse."

6.

As soon as it was dark they met on a street corner.

"I had to walk slowly," said Ken. "If you try to walk fast, this thing gets frisky."

"I'll carry it for a while."

"Have any trouble getting out?"

"Are you kidding?" said Mac. "With all the confusion there is in my house? I just faded. How about you?"

"No problem. My folks were having a bridge party, so when I told them I wanted to go over to see you they said okay." Not much went on around Ken's house that involved him, anyway. "They've got a crazy idea you're all right for me to pal around with.

Maybe when they come to get us tonight at the police station they'll change their minds."

"Aren't we lucky your father's a lawyer!" quipped Mac. "Still, the police will never arrest us. There won't be enough left to arrest after Rufus gets through with us!"

It was all very well to joke about things like that while they were walking along well-lighted streets in a more or less normal manner (the string bag *did* move in strange ways if not watched). But when they reached the cemetery wall and began looking for a place to climb over it under the cover of a tree and at a comfortable distance from a streetlight, their mood changed. At least Ken's did.

"We've got to move fast, when no cars are coming," he said nervously, watching one pass.

"You go first and I'll throw the bag over to you."

The street was clear and quiet. Ken scrambled up the rough stone wall, bellied down on top of it, and dropped over the other side, barking a shin in the process.

"Okay!" he called in a hoarse whisper.

Here came the bag, but it came like something in a slow-motion film. It looked the size of the moon as it floated lazily over the wall.

By that time Mac was already up and dropping down beside Ken.

A truck rumbled down the street, its headlights sliding along the top of the wall like searchlights probing walls in a prison-break movie. The "moon" set just in time, dropping seconds before the headlights could pick it up. Mac grabbed the bag.

"Phase Three completed," he muttered happily. "Operation Balloon Ascension is proceeding on schedule."

"I hope the cops don't decide to come in for a look around," said Ken. "I've seen them drive in here at night."

"Well, if they do they'll have to unlock the gates first and we'll hear them, so we'll have plenty of warning."

"I hope so!"

When the boys reached the gates of the right-of-way, Mac stopped.

"Okay, now, let's get everything ready. We don't want to be rattling a shopping bag right under their windows."

He held the string bag open wide, too wide.

The balloon rose, shopping bag and all.
  "Grab it!"

Ken grabbed wildly and caught the cord.

"Attaboy! Okay, pull her down and let's get that bag off."

When the balloon was in working order, Ken held it while Mac climbed to the top of the gates.

"We sure went to a lot of trouble getting *into* the cemetery just to get out of it again!" Ken grumbled.

"All in a night's work," said Mac cheerfully. "Hand me our secret weapon."

Ken handed the balloon string up to him and Mac made his way down the other side of the gates. Then Ken joined him. And he had no more than reached the ground when a sudden sound made his blood run cold. It was the thunderous, baying bark of a very large dog.

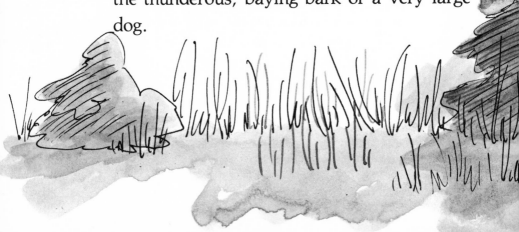

Ken stared at Mac, trembling. Even in the darkness Mac's face stood out clearly, maybe because it was so pale. But even then Mac managed a grin.

"That came from inside the house, so we're safe," he whispered. "Let's wait a few minutes. Give old Rufe a chance to settle down."

"Do you th-think he h-heard us?"

"Oh, he may have heard something, but if he doesn't hear anything more he'll settle down again and go back to sleep, or whatever he's doing."

"I hope you're right!"

At first Ken felt ready to wait for at least an hour. But then as the minutes dragged by and Rufus did not sound off again, suspense became worse than fear.

"How about it, Mac?"

"Okay. Now or never."

"Don't give me a choice."

48

An Indian would have envied the silence of their footsteps. They crept as silently as ghosts down the path between trees and bushes, holding the balloon low. Ahead of them the tall house loomed in the dark. A terrible thought occurred to Ken. What if they didn't have enough light to see by?

But then as they neared the jutting corner he began to have hope again. Light shone in a subdued way from the first-floor windows, and from the second floor, too. There was even a hint of light coming from high up through a third-floor window.

They had reached the corner of the house. Mac took the balloon and slowly began to pay out cord, easing it up alongside the house. Ken could see the white packet hanging down from the gutter and the hook it was hanging from.

It seemed to take Mac forever to work the wire loop in toward the hook. Would it catch?

Then from somewhere in front of the house

came a frightening sound — the sound of a
door being opened.

"All right, Rufus, go ahead, but make it
snappy!" said an impatient voice, while two
boys turned to jelly in the dark.

Even at such a moment, however, Mac could not give up. He managed one convulsive jerk on the cord.

The loop caught on the hook.

And the red balloon caught on the tin gutter.

BOOM!

In the stillness of the night the explosion sounded like a cannon. And Etta Simmons's voice sounded like a steam whistle.

"What was that?" she screamed.

"It came from upstairs!" cried Cyrus Simmons. "Rufus! Come back here! Rufus! Inside, sir! Now — upstairs, boy! Let's go!"

Tattered remnants of red and gray balloons hit the ground at the boys' feet. So did the packet. Mac scooped up everything and jammed the whole lot in his pocket. Through the open windows he and Ken could hear Rufus baying and feet clattering on stairs, but they did not linger to hear more.

7.

It felt good to be walking down a well-lighted street again. Ken was still twitching a little, but at least the seat of his pants was where it belonged.

"I think we'd better mail this to Mr. Swanson," said Mac, pulling the packet out of one pocket and an envelope out of the other. "If we took it to him he'd want to share it with us. And I'd expect him to, if he just wanted it for himself," he added severely, "but he didn't."

He put the packet inside and licked the flap and sealed it. Ken stared at the envelope. Then he grabbed it from Mac and took a closer look.

"You mean to tell me you brought along an envelope already stamped and addressed? You mean to tell me you were that sure we'd pull it off?"

Mac released one of his crazy chuckles.

"Well, you've got to have a little self-confidence in this world," he said. "If you don't have that, you don't have anything!"

As he retrieved the envelope from Ken's nerveless fingers, Ken burst out again.

"Now, wait a minute! You act as if you had masterminded the perfect crime — but what would have happened if that balloon hadn't burst when it did? Don't tell me you planned *that*!"

"Of course I did!"

"Baloney!"

Mac shrugged.

"Well, no, I didn't," he admitted, "but when you have enough self-confidence you always seem to get a little break here and there."

"A *little* break?" Ken could say no more. He was flabbergasted. And he was still in that condition when they came to a mailbox. Mac walked over to it. He held up the envelope and glanced at Ken.

"Okay with you?"

Ken looked at it and felt curiously light-hearted.

"Sure," he said, and laughed. "Well, at least I broke even on the deal — but you, you're out two bits plus postage!"

The Great McGoniggle's face twisted again with one of those lunatic grins.

"Then I'm ahead of the game. Because I got at least fifty cents' worth of fun out of it — maybe more!" he declared, and dropped the envelope in the box.

Books by Scott Corbett

The Trick Books

THE LEMONADE TRICK
THE MAILBOX TRICK
THE DISAPPEARING DOG TRICK
THE LIMERICK TRICK
THE BASEBALL TRICK
THE TURNABOUT TRICK
THE HAIRY HORROR TRICK
THE HATEFUL PLATEFUL TRICK
THE HOME RUN TRICK
THE HOCKEY TRICK

What Makes It Work?

WHAT MAKES A CAR GO?
WHAT MAKES A TV WORK?
WHAT MAKES A LIGHT GO ON?
WHAT MAKES A PLANE FLY?
WHAT MAKES A BOAT FLOAT?

Easy-to-Read Adventure Stories

DR. MERLIN'S MAGIC SHOP
THE GREAT CUSTARD PIE PANIC
THE BOY WHO WALKED ON AIR
THE GREAT McGONIGGLE'S GRAY GHOST

Suspense Stories

TREE HOUSE ISLAND
DEAD MAN'S LIGHT
CUTLASS ISLAND
ONE BY SEA
THE BASEBALL BARGAIN
THE MYSTERY MAN
THE CASE OF THE GONE GOOSE
THE CASE OF THE FUGITIVE FIREBUG
THE CASE OF THE TICKLISH TOOTH
THE RED ROOM RIDDLE
DEAD BEFORE DOCKING
RUN FOR THE MONEY
HERE LIES THE BODY
THE CASE OF THE SILVER SKULL
THE CASE OF THE BURGLED BLESSING BOX